OP

OLD HICKORY PRESS

For my grandboy,

Jackson

Published by
Old Hickory Press
PO Box 2
Versailles, KY 40383

ILLUSTRATION BY RON NOBLE

Printed in the United States of America
ISBN-13: 978-0-9996228-1-0
eBook ISBN-13: 978-0-9996228-2-7

Ralph Squirrels' family had a home in a tree
Next to the fairway and the 15th tee.

All his life he had watched people play the game
And he longed for the day when he could do the same.

"Practice makes perfect," Mama Squirrels told him
So Ralph would hit acorns with a fallen tree limb.

HOME SWEET HOME

Looking forward to the day, Ralph prayed in his soul,
When he could tee up a ball and knock it in the hole.

Then one day he heard the course would be closed
To fix something wrong with a watering hose.

And that his animal friends were wanting to play
A big round of golf on the course that day!

Golf Course
CLOSED
For Repairs

There was Dinker the duck and a rabbit named Rab
Toby the Turtle and Crabby the Crab.

A skunk named Stinker and Cackle the Crow
They all got together and were ready to go.

No one had ever really played golf before
But they knew what to do when a player yelled "Fore!"

They knew that it meant to get out of the way
When one of their buddies hit it astray.

FORE!

Ralph had studied their moves and knew what not to do
And he had practiced his swing 'til he pretty well knew

That he could be good at this new game he'd found
If he only got to play a couple of rounds.

Ralph was excited and anxious to play
And nervous in front of his friends that way.

But Ralph knew to play well on that very first tee
He had to be calm and cool as could be.

There was one thing Ralph didn't foresee
How playing golf with his friends would be.

And he soon found out that what they all lacked
Was knowing how golfers are supposed to act.

Toby took his time with his slow steady gait.
Didn't seem to mind making everybody wait.

And Rab was so fast scurrying around
Hopping to every shot before it even hit the ground.

Cackle was loud, obnoxious and rude
Ruining all the fun with his bad attitude.

Crabby was cranky getting stuck in the sand
Over and over, not what he had planned.

"Quack, quack," said Dinker when he dunked it in the pond.
Cackle laughed and made fun of what he'd done.

Stinker and Rab and the rest joined in
But Ralph encouraged Dinker, saying "Try it again."

And his next shot flew high straight to the green
"Good shot," said Ralph, "See what I mean?"

You have to shut out the noise, maintain your poise
And focus on making the shot.

Imagine the ball flying through the air
And landing in just the right spot."

Ralph put an acorn on top of the tee
Stepped back closed his eyes and in his mind he could see

Exactly where he wanted his shot to land
Then he looked down at a real golf club in his hand,

And the acorn on the tee became a real golf ball
And Ralph didn't hear any of the noise at all.

As he addressed the ball and took his stance
It felt like he was in some sort of a trance.

Then he made his shot with a smooth easy swing
And he flew with the ball all the way to the green.

18

It was straight at the flag and with a bounce and a roll,
Like it had its own eyes plunked right in the hole.

Ralph and his friends couldn't believe what they'd seen
So as fast as they could they all ran to the green.

Ralph got there first, reached into the cup
And to his surprise picked an acorn up.

And the club in his hand was again the long stick.
The round was over and it ended too quick.

Ralph couldn't wait to tee it up again
And play on the course with all of his friends.

And through all the noise, the joy and the fun
Maybe hit another hole-in-one!

But in the meantime he could practice his swing
And dream about the ball landing on the green.

Because Ralph learned something real important that day
That in his imagination he could always play.

CPSIA information can be obtained at www.ICGtesting.com
Printed in the USA
LVIW012319040820
662292LV00011B/254

9 780999 622810